HUG?

Charlene Chua

Kids Can Press

GULP!

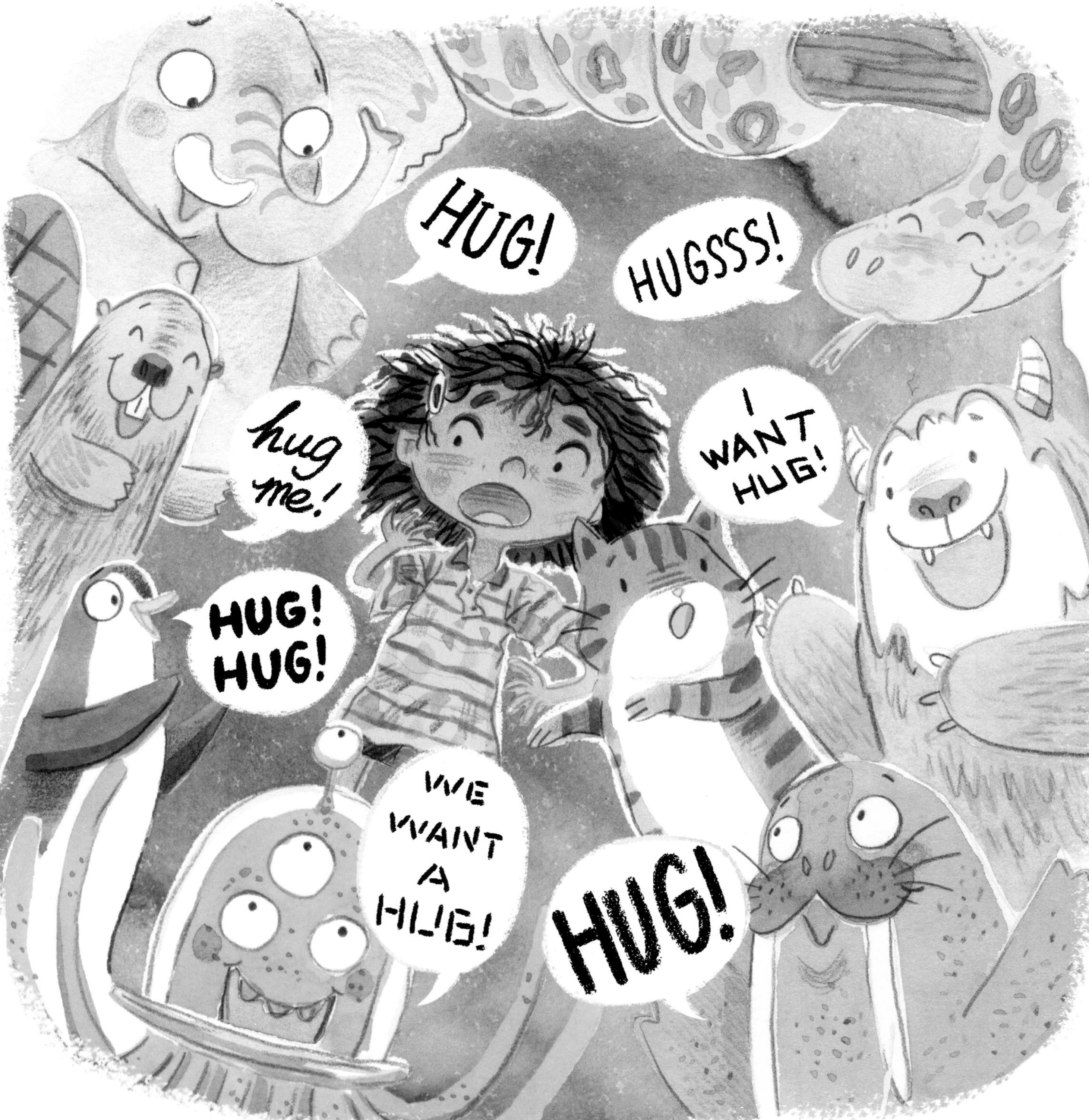
HUG!
HUGSSS!
hug me!
I WANT HUG!
HUG! HUG!
WE WANT A HUG!
HUG!

Hugs are great.

For Uno — hugs forever, sweet princess

Kids Can Press gratefully acknowledges the financial support of the Government of Ontario, through Ontario Creates; the Ontario Arts Council; the Canada Council for the Arts; and the Government of Canada for our publishing activity.

Published in Canada and the U.S. by Kids Can Press Ltd.
25 Dockside Drive, Toronto, ON M5A 0B5

Kids Can Press is a Corus Entertainment Inc. company

www.kidscanpress.com

The artwork in this book was rendered in watercolor, watercolor ink and colored pencil, then scanned and digitally manipulated in Photoshop.
The text is set in Borrowdale.

Edited by Jennifer Stokes
Designed by Michael Reis

Printed and bound in Buji, Shenzhen, China, in 04/2020 by WKT Company

CM 20 0 9 8 7 6 5 4 3 2 1

FSC
www.fsc.org
MIX
Paper from
responsible sources
FSC® C010256

Library and Archives Canada Cataloguing in Publication

Title: Hug? / Charlene Chua.
Names: Chua, Charlene, author, illustrator.
Identifiers: Canadiana 20190201584 | ISBN 9781525302060 (hardcover)
Subjects: LCGFT: Picture books.
Classification: LCC PS8605.H825 H84 2020 | DDC jC813/.6 — dc23